US MILITARY EQUIPMENT
AND VEHICLES

# US AIR FORCE
## EQUIPMENT AND VEHICLES

BY ARNOLD RINGSTAD

CONTENT CONSULTANT
CAPTAIN KYLE P. ESQUIBEL
ASSISTANT PROFESSOR OF MILITARY SCIENCE
GONZAGA ARMY ROTC

Kids Core
An Imprint of Abdo Publishing
abdobooks.com

# abdobooks.com

Published by Abdo Publishing, a division of ABDO, PO Box 398166, Minneapolis, Minnesota 55439. Copyright © 2022 by Abdo Consulting Group, Inc. International copyrights reserved in all countries. No part of this book may be reproduced in any form without written permission from the publisher. Kids Core™ is a trademark and logo of Abdo Publishing.

Printed in the United States of America, North Mankato, Minnesota
052021
092021

**THIS BOOK CONTAINS RECYCLED MATERIALS**

Cover Photo: Senior Airman Alexander Cook/US Air Force
Interior Photos: Senior Airman Justin Hodge/US Air National Guard, 4–5, 29 (top); Tech. Sgt. Dana Rosso/US Air Force, 6; Senior Airman Alexander Cook/US Air Force, 9; Airman 1st Class Alexander Cook/US Air Force, 10; Senior Airman John Linzmeier/ US Air Force/Defense Visual Information Distribution Service, 12–13, 28; Jim Haseltine/US Air Force, 14; Senior Airman Hayden Legg/US Air Force/Defense Visual Information Distribution Service, 15; Master Sgt. Jeffrey Allen/US Air Force, 17; Airman Zoe T. Perkins/US Air Force/Defense Visual Information Distribution Service, 18; Staff Sgt. Timothy Mesko/US Air National Guard/ Defense Visual Information Distribution Service, 20–21; Staff Sgt. Jeremy M. Wilson/US Air Force, 23, 29 (bottom); Shutterstock Images, 24 (left), 24 (top right), 24 (middle right); Victor Metelskiy/Shutterstock Images, 24 (bottom right); Airman 1st Class Nicole Molignano/US Air Force/Defense Visual Information Distribution Service, 26

Editor: Katharine Hale
Series Designer: Jake Nordby

**Library of Congress Control Number: 2020948340**

**Publisher's Cataloging-in-Publication Data**

Names: Ringstad, Arnold, author.
Title: US Air Force equipment and vehicles / by Arnold Ringstad
Description: Minneapolis, Minnesota : Abdo Publishing, 2022 | Series: US military equipment and vehicles | Includes online resources and index.
Identifiers: ISBN 9781532195433 (lib. bdg.) | ISBN 9781644946169 (pbk.) | ISBN 9781098215743 (ebook)
Subjects: LCSH: Air forces--Juvenile literature. | United States. Air Force--Facilities--Juvenile literature. | United States. Air Force-- Supplies and stores--Juvenile literature. | Vehicles, Military--Juvenile literature. | Military supplies--Juvenile literature. | Military paraphernalia--Juvenile literature.
Classification: DDC 623.7--dc23

# CONTENTS

The United States is the only country to use the F-22 Raptor.

# CHAPTER 1

# FLY, FIGHT, WIN

Four F-22 Raptors were going on a mission. Raptors are fighter aircraft. They can shoot **missiles** at enemy planes. They can also drop bombs on ground targets.

The Raptor's shape and paint help it hide from enemies.

The Raptor was the right plane for the job.
The mission was in a country that had powerful
surface-to-air missiles (SAMs). These missiles
shoot down airplanes. SAMs use radar to
see their targets. Radar equipment sends out

radio waves. Those waves bounce off distant objects, such as airplanes. The equipment senses the reflections.

The Raptor is a **stealth** aircraft. It is designed to hide from radar. It is shaped so radio waves reflect in all directions, not back to the radar equipment. Special paint on its skin also absorbs radio waves.

The Raptors soared into the mission area. No SAMs were fired at them. The pilots found their target. Then they dropped bombs. The building exploded, and the mission was a success. The US Air Force pilots returned to base safely.

# What Is the Air Force?

The US Air Force is part of the US military. It is one of six branches of the military. Its goal is to protect the United States in the air. Part of its motto is "Fly, Fight, Win."

## A New Branch

In 2019, the US military formed a sixth branch. It is called the US Space Force. Before, the US Air Force carried out missions in space. It launched satellites. These spacecraft are used for communication, reconnaissance, and other purposes. The US Space Force has taken over these missions.

Mechanics, technicians, navigators, and others play an important role in helping air force planes fly.

As jets approach the speed of sound, they can create shock waves called vapor cones.

The US Air Force does many kinds of missions. Different kinds of equipment and vehicles help it carry out those missions. The equipment and vehicles of the US Air Force allow the branch to fly, fight, and win.

Major Paul Lopez II is a Raptor pilot in the US Air Force. In an interview, he talked about what makes the Raptor such a powerful plane:

> The F-22 Raptor is an air dominance fighter. It's capable of flying twice the speed of sound, up to 60,000 feet [18,000 m] high, and we are extremely maneuverable.

Source: "US Air Force: Maj Paul Lopez II, F-22 Pilot." *YouTube*, uploaded by US Air Force and Space Force Recruiting, 11 Oct. 2017, youtube.com. Accessed 22 May 2020.

## What's the Big Idea?

Read this quote carefully. What is its main idea? Explain how the main idea is supported by details.

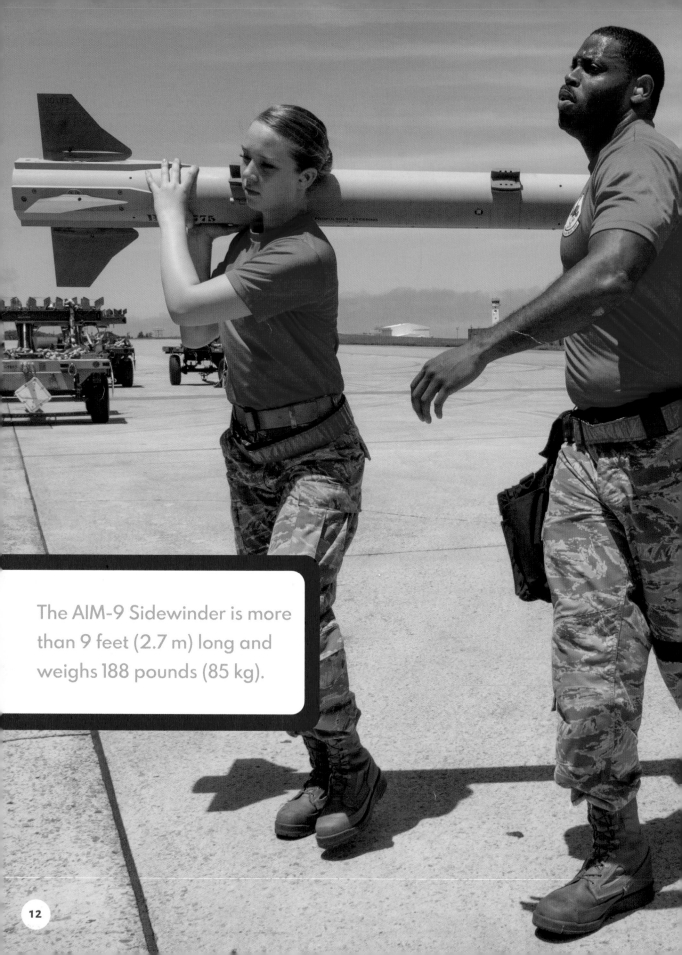

The AIM-9 Sidewinder is more than 9 feet (2.7 m) long and weighs 188 pounds (85 kg).

# CHAPTER 2

# WEAPONS AND GEAR

Some air force missiles are designed to shoot down enemy aircraft. One example is the AIM-9 Sidewinder. The Sidewinder is a heat-seeking missile. It detects the heat from enemy aircraft. Then it flies toward the aircraft and explodes.

The F-35 is one type of fighter jet that uses the GBU-12 Paveway II.

Air force planes drop bombs on ground targets. The GBU-12 Paveway II is one of these bombs. The pilot aims a laser at the target. Then the bomb falls from the aircraft. Fins spring out from the bomb's sides. They move to steer the

Though machine guns are not used often, they are installed on some aircraft.

bomb in the air. The bomb can sense the laser. It follows the laser to the target.

Some air force planes also carry machine guns. This lets airmen fight at close range. However, the guns are rarely used. Today, pilots mostly fight using missiles. They shoot their targets from many miles away. They do not get close enough to fire the guns.

# Flight Gear

Flying planes can be tough on a pilot's body. Planes may turn and roll at high speeds. Sometimes this can make the pilot's blood rush down to the legs. The brain does not get enough blood. If this happens, the pilot may pass out. To avoid that, pilots wear G suits. These suits squeeze the lower body. They help keep

## Survival Equipment

Pilots may have to make emergency landings in dangerous places. The landscape or weather could be harsh. There could be enemy soldiers around. Pilots have survival gear in the cockpit. This gear includes medical supplies, a life raft, and tools. It even has a gun.

Equipment such as G suits and oxygen masks help keep pilots safe.

blood in the pilot's head. The pilot can keep flying safely.

Oxygen masks are also important gear. The air is thin at high **altitudes**. There is little oxygen to breathe. When there is little oxygen, people can have trouble thinking. They can even pass out. Oxygen masks give pilots plenty of oxygen.

Pilots learn how to attach the harness of an ejector seat so it can keep them safe if needed.

If there is an emergency, a pilot may need to escape a plane quickly. This is what ejection seats are for. When there is a problem, the pilot pulls a handle. The top of the cockpit blows off. Rockets in the seat fire. They carry the pilot away from the plane. Then parachutes in the seat **deploy**. The pilot is able to land safely.

## Explore Online

Visit the website below. Does it give any new information about being a fighter pilot that wasn't in Chapter Two?

### What's It like to Be a Fighter Pilot?

abdocorelibrary.com/air-force -equipment-vehicles

The F-22, *bottom*, and F-35, *middle*, are modern stealth fighters. The P-51 Mustang, *top*, is a plane from World War II.

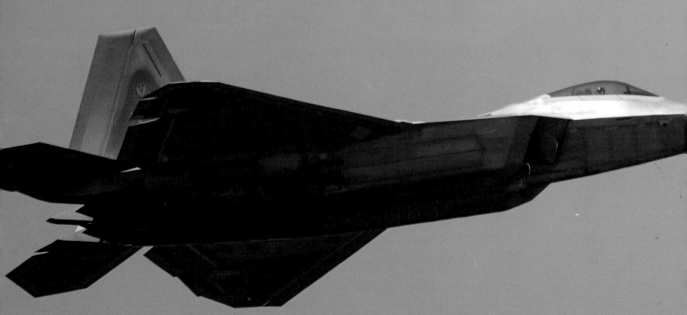

# CHAPTER 3

# THE PLANES OF THE AIR FORCE

Fighter jets are some of the most famous planes in the world. They are sleek and fast. The F-22 Raptor is a top fighter jet in the US Air Force. This plane is a stealth fighter. The Raptor joined the air force in 2005. It still rules the sky.

The F-35 Lightning II is a newer fighter. It is smaller and cheaper than the Raptor. But it also uses stealth. The Lightning II is known for its advanced computers and sensors. The plane can warn pilots of enemy planes and missiles. Pilots wear a special helmet. It shows them the information the plane is taking in. This gives pilots a better view of the battle around them.

## Bombers

Some fighter jets can drop bombs. But that is not a fighter jet's main job. Other planes are made just for bombing. They can carry lots of bombs at once. They are called bombers.

The most advanced bomber is the B-2 Spirit. Like the Raptor and Lightning II, it is a

Two pilots work together to fly a B-2.

stealth aircraft. The B-2 has an unusual shape.
It looks like a big flying wing. It has no tail. Its
shape helps the B-2 go undetected.

# How Big Are US Air Force Aircraft?

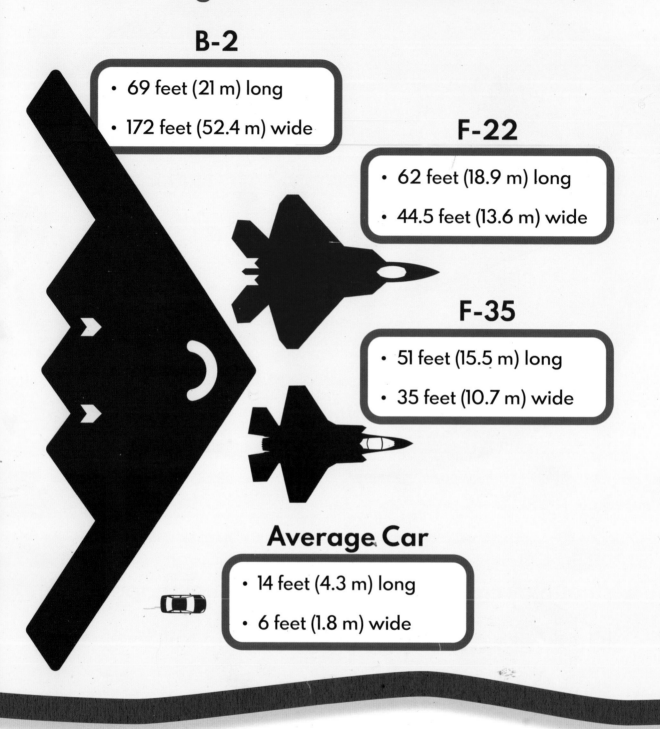

### B-2
- 69 feet (21 m) long
- 172 feet (52.4 m) wide

### F-22
- 62 feet (18.9 m) long
- 44.5 feet (13.6 m) wide

### F-35
- 51 feet (15.5 m) long
- 35 feet (10.7 m) wide

### Average Car
- 14 feet (4.3 m) long
- 6 feet (1.8 m) wide

This diagram compares the sizes of a few US Air Force aircraft. It also shows the size of a normal car.

# Cargo Planes

Not all of the air force's planes are for fighting. Some carry **cargo** or troops instead. They bring supplies to troops fighting on the ground.

One of the air force's cargo planes is the C-17 Globemaster III. It has four huge engines and space for lots of cargo. The plane can fit 102 parachute troops with their gear. It can even carry tanks.

## UAVs

Some US Air Force planes don't have pilots inside. These are called unmanned aerial vehicles (UAVs). Pilots control them from the ground. One of these UAVs is the MQ-9 Reaper. It can fire missiles at ground targets below. Another UAV is the RQ-4 Global Hawk. The Global Hawk gathers information.

The C-5 Galaxy is one of the largest aircraft in the world.

For the biggest cargo, the military uses the C-5 Galaxy. It is longer, wider, and taller than the C-17. It can also hold about 100,000 pounds (45,000 kg) more cargo than the C-17.

# Flying and Fighting

The air force's fighter jets zoom into battle and fire missiles. Its stealthy bombers soar overhead and drop bombs. And its cargo planes help support troops on the ground. The US Air Force's equipment and vehicles make it the strongest air force in the world.

## Further Evidence

Look at the website below. What evidence from the site supports what you learned in Chapter Three?

## B-2 Spirit

abdocorelibrary.com/air-force -equipment-vehicles

# IMPORTANT GEAR

## AIM-9 Sidewinder

- Heat-seeking missile
- Detects the heat given off by enemy aircraft

# F-22 Raptor

- Stealth fighter aircraft
- Fights enemy aircraft and drops bombs

# B-2 Spirit

- Stealth bomber aircraft
- Drops laser-guided bombs
- Shaped like a large flying wing

# Glossary

**altitudes**
various heights in the air above sea level

**cargo**
supplies that planes carry, including equipment
and vehicles

**deploy**
to spread out or send out

**missiles**
weapons that use their own engines to fly toward targets

**motto**
a saying that is used to represent a group

**reconnaissance**
the act of collecting information

**satellites**
spacecraft that circle larger bodies in space, such as Earth

**stealth**
designed in a way to hide from radar

# Online Resources

To learn more about US Air Force equipment and vehicles, visit our free resource websites below.

Visit **abdocorelibrary.com** or scan this QR code for free Common Core resources for teachers and students, including vetted activities, multimedia, and booklinks, for deeper subject comprehension.

Visit **abdobooklinks.com** or scan this QR code for free additional online weblinks for further learning. These links are routinely monitored and updated to provide the most current information available.

# Learn More

Bassier, Emma. *Military Aircraft.* Abdo Publishing, 2020.

McCarthy, Cecilia Pinto. *Military Drones.*
Abdo Publishing, 2021.

# Index

# About the Author

Arnold Ringstad has written more than 100 books for young readers. He lives in Minnesota with his wife and their cat. He enjoys visiting museums to see amazing military aircraft in person.